Leonid Andreyev

Love of One´s Neighbor

Salzwasser

Leonid Andreyev

Love of One´s Neighbor

1. Auflage | ISBN: 978-3-84604-868-9

Erscheinungsort: Frankfurt, Deutschland

Erscheinungsjahr: 2020

Salzwasser Verlag GmbH

Reprint of the original, first published in 1914.

LOVE OF ONE'S NEIGHBOR

LOVE OF ONE'S NEIGHBOR

BY

LEONID ANDREYEV

AUTHORIZED TRANSLATION BY

THOMAS SELTZER

NEW YORK
ALBERT AND CHARLES BONI
96 FIFTH AVENUE
1914

LOVE OF ONE'S NEIGHBOR

SCENE.　*A wild place in the mountains.*

(A man in an attitude of despair is standing on a tiny projection of a rock that rises almost sheer from the ground. How he got there it is not easy to say, but he cannot be reached either from above or below. Short ladders, ropes and sticks show that attempts have been made to save the unknown person, but without success.

It seems that the unhappy man has been in that desperate position a long time. A considerable crowd has already collected, extremely varied in composition. There are venders of cold drinks; there is a whole little bar behind which the bartender skips about out of breath and perspiring—he has more on his hands than he can attend to; there are peddlers selling picture postal cards, coral beads, souvenirs, and all sorts of trash. One fellow is stubbornly trying to dispose of a tortoise-shell comb, which is really not tortoise-shell. Tourists keep pouring in from all sides, attracted by the report that a catastrophe is impending—Englishmen, Americans, Germans, Russians, Frenchmen, Italians, etc., with all their peculiar national traits of character, manner and dress. Nearly all carry alpenstocks, field-glasses and cameras. The conversation is in different languages, all of which, for the convenience of the reader, we shall translate into English.

At the foot of the rock where the unknown man is to fall, two policemen are chasing the children away and partitioning off a space, drawing a rope around short stakes stuck in the ground. It is noisy and jolly.)

POLICEMAN. Get away, you loafer! The man'll fall on your head and then your mother and father will be making a hullabaloo about it.

BOY. Will he fall here?

POLICEMAN. Yes, here.

BOY. Suppose he drops farther?

SECOND POLICEMAN. The boy is right. He may get desperate and jump, land beyond the rope and hit some people in the crowd. I guess he weighs at least about two hundred pounds.

FIRST POLICEMAN. Move on, move on, you! Where are you going? Is that your daughter, lady? Please take her away! The young man will soon fall.

LADY. Soon? Did you say he is going to fall soon? Oh, heavens, and my husband's not here!

LITTLE GIRL. He's in the café, mamma.

LADY (*desperately*). Yes, of course. He's always in the café. Go call him, Nellie. Tell him the man will soon drop. Hurry! Hurry!

VOICES. Waiter! — Garçon — Kellner—Three beers out here!—No beer?—What?—Say, that's a fine bar—We'll have some in a moment—Hurry up—Waiter!—Waiter!—Garçon!

FIRST POLICEMAN. Say, boy, you're here again?

BOY. I wanted to take the stone away.

POLICEMAN. What for?

BOY. So he shouldn't get hurt so badly when he falls.

SECOND POLICEMAN. The boy is right. We ought to remove the stone. We ought to clear the place altogether. Isn't there any sawdust or sand about?

(*Two English tourists enter. They look at the unknown man through field-glasses and exchange remarks.*)

FIRST TOURIST. He's young.

SECOND TOURIST. How old?

FIRST TOURIST. Twenty-eight.

SECOND TOURIST. Twenty-six. Fright has made him look older.

FIRST TOURIST. How much will you bet?

SECOND TOURIST. Ten to a hundred. Put it down.

FIRST TOURIST (*writing in his note-book. To the policeman*). How did he got up there? Why don't they take him off?

POLICEMAN. They tried, but they couldn't. Our ladders are too short.

SECOND TOURIST. Has he been here long?

POLICEMAN. Two days.

FIRST TOURIST. Aha! He'll drop at night.

SECOND TOURIST. In two hours. A hundred to a hundred.

FIRST TOURIST. Put it down. (*He shouts to the man on the rock.*) How are you feeling? What? I can't hear you.

UNKNOWN MAN (*in a scarcely audible voice*). Bad, very bad.

LADY. Oh, heavens, and my husband is not here!

LITTLE GIRL (*running in*). Papa said he'll get here in plenty of time. He's playing chess.

LADY. Oh, heavens! Nellie, tell him he must come. I insist. But perhaps I had rather— Will he fall soon, Mr. Policeman? No? Nellie, you go. I'll stay here and keep the place for papa.

(*A tall, lanky woman of unusually independent*

and military appearance and a tourist dispute for the same place. The tourist, a short, quiet, rather weak man, feebly defends his rights; the woman is resolute and aggressive.)

TOURIST. But, lady, it is my place. I have been standing here for two hours.

MILITARY WOMAN. What do I care how long you have been standing here. I want this place. Do you understand? It offers a good view, and that's just what I want. Do you understand?

TOURIST (*weakly*). It's what I want, too.

MILITARY WOMAN. I beg your pardon, what do you know about these things anyway?

TOURIST. What knowledge is required? A man will fall. That's all.

MILITARY WOMAN (*mimicking*). "A man will fall. That's all." Won't you have the goodness to tell me whether you have ever seen a man fall? No? Well, I did. Not one, but three. Two acrobats, one rope-walker and three aeronauts.

TOURIST. That makes six.

MILITARY WOMAN (*mimicking*). "That makes six." Say, you are a mathematical prodigy. And did you ever see a tiger tear a woman to pieces in a zoo, right before your eyes? Eh? What? Yes, exactly. Now, I did— Please! Please!

(*The tourist steps aside, shrugging his shoulders*

with an air of injury, and the tall woman triumphantly takes possession of the stone she has won by her prowess. She sits down, spreading out around her her bag, handkerchiefs, peppermints, and medicine bottle, takes off her gloves and wipes her field-glass, glancing pleasantly on all around. Finally she turns to the lady who is waiting for her husband in the café.)

MILITARY WOMAN (*amiably*). You will tire yourself out, dear. Why don't you sit down?

LADY. Oh, my, don't talk about it. My legs are as stiff as that rock there.

MILITARY WOMAN. Men are so rude nowadays. They will never give their place to a woman. Have you brought peppermints with you?

LADY (*frightened*). No. Why? Is it necessary?

MILITARY WOMAN. When you keep looking up a long time you are bound to get sick. Sure thing. Have you spirits of ammonia? No? Good gracious, how thoughtless! How will they bring you back to consciousness when he falls? You haven't any smelling salts either, I dare say. Of course not. Have you anybody to take care of you, seeing that you are so helpless yourself?

LADY (*frightened*). I will tell my husband. He is in the café.

MILITARY WOMAN. Your husband is a brute.

POLICEMAN. Whose coat is this? Who threw this rag here?

BOY. It's mine. I spread my coat there so that he doesn't hurt himself so badly when he falls.

POLICEMAN. Take it away.

(*Two tourists armed with cameras contending for the same position.*)

FIRST TOURIST. I wanted this place.

SECOND TOURIST. You wanted it, but I got it.

FIRST TOURIST. You just came here. I have had this place for two days.

SECOND TOURIST. Then why did you go without even leaving your shadow?

FIRST TOURIST. I wasn't going to starve myself to death.

COMB-VENDER (*mysteriously*). Tortoise-shell.

TOURIST (*savagely*). Well?

VENDOR. Genuine tortoise-shell.

TOURIST. Go to the devil.

THIRD TOURIST, PHOTOGRAPHER. For heaven's sake, lady, you're sitting on my camera!

LITTLE LADY. Oh! Where is it?

TOURIST. Under you, under you, lady.

LITTLE LADY. I am so tired. What a wretched camera you have. I thought it felt uncomfortable and I was wondering why. Now I know; I am sitting on your camera.

TOURIST (*agonized*). Lady!

LITTLE LADY. I thought it was a stone. I saw something lying there and I thought: A queer-looking stone; I wonder why it's so black. So that's what it was; it was your camera. I see.

TOURIST (*agonized*). Lady, for heaven's sake!

LITTLE LADY. Why is it so large, tell me. Cameras are small, but this one is so large. I swear I never had the faintest suspicion it was a camera. Can you take my picture? I would so much like to have my picture taken with the mountains here for a background, in this wonderful setting.

TOURIST. How can I take your picture if you are sitting on my camera?

LITTLE LADY (*jumping up, frightened*). Is it possible? You don't say so. Why didn't you tell me so? Does it take pictures?

VOICES. Waiter, one beer!—What did you bring wine for?—I gave you my order long ago.—What will you have, sir?—One minute.—In a second. Waiter!—Waiter—Toothpicks!—

(*A fat tourist enters in haste, panting, surrounded by a numerous family.*)

TOURIST (*crying*). Mary! Aleck! Jimmie!— Where is Mary? For God's sake! Where is Mary?

STUDENT (*dismally*). Here she is, papa.

TOURIST. Where is she? Mary!

GIRL. Here I am, papa.

TOURIST. Where in the world are you? (*He turns around.*) Ah, there! What are you standing back of me for? Look, look! For goodness sake, where are you looking?

GIRL (*dismally*). I don't know, papa.

TOURIST. No, that's impossible. Imagine! She never once saw a lightning flash. She always keeps her eyes open as wide as onions, but the instant it flashes she closes them. So she never saw lightning, not once. Mary, you are missing it again. There it is! You see!

STUDENT. She sees, papa.

TOURIST. Keep an eye on her. (*Suddenly dropping into tone of profound pity.*) Ah, poor young man. Imagine! He'll fall from that high rock. Look, children, see how pale he is! That should be a lesson to you how dangerous climbing is.

STUDENT (*dismally*). He won't fall to-day, papa!

SECOND GIRL. Papa, Mary has closed her eyes again.

FIRST STUDENT. Let us sit down, papa! Upon my word, he won't fall to-day. The porter told me so. I can't stand it any more. You've been dragging us about every day from morning till night visiting art galleries.

TOURIST. What's that? For whose benefit am I doing this? Do you think I enjoy spending my time with a dunce?

SECOND GIRL. Papa, Mary is blinking her eyes again.

SECOND STUDENT. I can't stand it either. I have terrible dreams. Yesterday I dreamed of garçons the whole night long.

TOURIST. Jimmie.

FIRST STUDENT. I have gotten so thin I am nothing but skin and bones. I can't stand it any more, father. I'd rather be a farmer, or tend pigs.

TOURIST. Aleck.

FIRST STUDENT. If he were really to fall—but it's a fake. You believe every lie told you! They all lie. Baedecker lies, too. Yes, your Baedecker lies!

MARY (*dismally*). Papa, children, he's beginning to fall.

(*The man on the rock shouts something down into the crowd. There is general commotion. Voices, "Look, he's falling." Field-glasses are raised; the photographers, violently agitated, click their cameras; the policemen diligently clean the place where he is to fall.*)

PHOTOGRAPHER. Oh, hang it! What is the matter with me? The devil! When a man's in a hurry—

SECOND PHOTOGRAPHER. Brother, your camera is closed.

PHOTOGRAPHER. The devil take it.

VOICES. Hush! He's getting ready to fall.—No, he's saying something.—No, he's falling.—Hush!

UNKNOWN MAN ON THE ROCK (*faintly*). Save me! Save me!

TOURIST. Ah, poor young man. Mary, Jimmie, there's a tragedy for you. The sky is clear, the weather is beautiful, and has he to fall and be shattered to death? Can you realize how dreadful that is, Aleck?

STUDENT (*wearily*). Yes, I can realize it.

TOURIST. Mary, can you realize it? Imagine. There is the sky. There are people enjoying themselves and partaking of refreshments. Everything is no nice and pleasant, and he has to fall. What a tragedy! Do you remember Hamlet?

SECOND GIRL (*prompting*). Hamlet, Prince of Denmark, of Alsinore.

JAMES. Of Helsingfors, I know. Don't bother me, father!

MARY (*dismally*). He dreamed about garçons all night long.

ALECK. Why don't you order sandwiches, father.

COMB-VENDER (*mysteriously*). Tortoise-shell. Genuine tortoise-shell.

TOURIST (*credulously*). Stolen?

VENDOR. Why, sir, the idea!

TOURIST (*angrily*). Do you mean to tell me it's genuine if it isn't stolen? Go on. Not much.

MILITARY WOMAN (*amiably*). Are all these your children?

TOURIST. Yes, madam. A father's duty. You see, they are protesting. It is the eternal conflict between fathers and children. Here is such a tragedy going on, such a heart-rending tragedy— Mary, you are blinking your eyes again.

MILITARY WOMAN. You are quite right. Children must be hardened to things. But why do you call this a terrible tragedy? Every roofer, when he falls, falls from a great height. But this here—what is it? A hundred, two hundred feet. I saw a man fall plumb from the sky.

TOURIST (*overwhelmed*). You don't say?

ALECK. Children, listen. Plumb from the sky.

MILITARY WOMAN. Yes, yes. I saw an aeronaut drop from the clouds and go crash upon an iron roof.

TOURIST. How terrible!

MILITARY WOMAN. That's what I call a tragedy. It took two hours to bring me back to consciousness, and all that time they pumped water on me, the scoundrels. I was nearly drowned. From that day on I never step out of the door without taking spirits of ammonia with me.

(*Enter a strolling troop of Italian singers and musicians: a short, fat tenor, with a reddish beard and large, watery, stupidly dreamy eyes, singing with extraordinary sweetness; a skinny humpback with a jockey cap, and a screeching baritone; a bass who is also a mandolinist, looking like a bandit; a girl with a violin, closing her eyes when she plays, so that only the whites are seen. They take their stand and begin to sing: "Sul mare lucica—Santa Lucia, Santa Lucia—"*)

MARY (*dismally*). Papa, children, look. He is beginning to wave his hands.

TOURIST. Is that the effect the music has upon him?

MILITARY WOMAN. Quite possible. Music usually goes with such things. But that'll make him fall sooner than he should. Musicians, go away from here! Go!

(*A tall tourist, with up-curled mustache, violently gesticulating, enters, followed by a small group attracted by curiosity.*)

TALL TOURIST. It's scandalous. Why don't they save him? Ladies and gentlemen, you all heard him shout: "Save me." Didn't you?

THE CURIOUS (*in chorus*). Yes, yes, we heard him.

TALL TOURIST. There you are. I distinctly heard these words: "Save me! Why don't they save me?" It's scandalous. Policemen, policemen! Why don't you save him? What are you doing there?

POLICEMEN. We are cleaning up the place for him to fall.

TALL TOURIST. That's a sensible thing to do, too. But why don't you save him? You ought to save him. If a man asks you to save him, it is absolutely essential to save him. Isn't it so, ladies and gentlemen?

THE CURIOUS (*in chorus*). True, absolutely true. It is essential to save him.

TALL TOURIST (*with heat*). We are not heathens, we are Christians. We should love our neighbors. When a man asks to be saved every measure which the government has at its command should be taken to save him. Policemen, have you taken every measure?

POLICEMAN. Every one!

TALL TOURIST. Every one without exception? Gentleman, every measure has been taken. Listen, young man, every measure has been taken to save you. Did you hear?

UNKNOWN MAN (*in a scarcely audible voice*). Save me!

TALL TOURIST (*excitedly*). Gentlemen, did you hear? He again asked to be saved. Policemen, did you hear?

ONE OF THE CURIOUS (*timidly*). It is my opinion that it is absolutely necessary to save him.

TALL TOURIST. That's right. Exactly. Why, that's what I have been saying for the last two hours. Policemen, do you hear? It is scandalous.

ONE OF THE CURIOUS (*a little bolder*). It is my opinion that an appeal should be made to the highest authority.

THE REST (*in chorus*). Yes, yes, a complaint should be made. It is scandalous. The government ought not to leave any of its citizens in danger. We all pay taxes. He must be saved.

TALL TOURIST. Didn't I say so? Of course we must put up a complaint. Young man! Listen, young man. Do you pay taxes? What? I can't hear.

TOURIST. Jimmie, Katie, listen! What a tragedy! Ah, the poor young man! He is soon to fall and they ask him to pay a domiciliary tax.

KATE (*the girl with glasses, pedantically*). That can hardly be called a domicile, father. The meaning of domicile is—

JAMES (*pinching her*). Lickspittle.

MARY (*wearily*). Papa, children, look! He's again beginning to fall.

(*There is excitement in the crowd, and again a bustling and shouting among the photographers.*)

TALL TOURIST. We must hurry, ladies and gentlemen. He must be saved at any cost. Who's going with me?

THE CURIOUS (*in chorus*). We are all going! We are all going?

TALL TOURIST. Policemen, did you hear? Come, ladies and gentlemen!

(*They depart, fiercely gesticulating. The café grows more lively. The sound of clinking beer glasses and the clatter of steins is heard, and the beginning of a loud German song. The bartender, who has forgotten himself while talking to somebody, starts suddenly and runs off, looks up to the sky with a hopeless air and wipes the perspiration from his face with his napkin. Angry calls of Waiter! Waiter!*)

UNKNOWN MAN (*rather loudly*). Can you let me have some soda water?

(*The waiter is startled, looks at the sky, glances at the man on the rock, and pretending not to have heard him, walks away.*)

MANY VOICES. Waiter! Beer!

WAITER. One moment, one moment!

(*Two drunken men come out from the café.*)

LADY. Ah, there is my husband. Come here quick.

MILITARY WOMAN. A downright brute.

DRUNKEN MAN (*waving his hand to the unknown man*). Say, is it very bad up there? Hey?

UNKNOWN MAN (*rather loudly*). Yes, it's bad. I am sick and tired of it.

DRUNKEN MAN. Can't you get a drink?

UNKNOWN MAN. No, how can I?

SECOND DRUNKEN MAN. Say, what are you talking about? How can he get a drink? The man is about to die and you tempt him and try to get him excited. Listen, up there, we have been drinking your health right along. It won't hurt you, will it?

FIRST DRUNKEN MAN. Ah, go on! What are you talking about? How can it hurt him? Why, it will only do him good. It will encourage him. Listen, honest to God, we are very sorry for you, but don't mind us. We are going to the café to have another drink. Good-bye.

SECOND DRUNKEN MAN. Look, what a crowd.

FIRST DRUNKEN MAN. Come, or he'll fall and then they'll close the café.

(*Enter a new crowd of tourists, a very elegant gentleman, the chief correspondent of European newspapers at their head. He is followed by an ecstatic whisper of respect and admiration. Many leave the café to look at him, and even the waiter turns slightly around, glances at him quickly, smiles happily and continues on his way, spilling something from his tray.*)

VOICES. The correspondent! The correspondent! Look!

LADY. Oh, my, and my husband is gone again!

TOURIST. Jimmie, Mary, Aleck, Katie, Charlie, look! This is the chief correspondent. Do you realize it? The very highest of all. Whatever he writes goes.

KATE. Mary, dear, again you are not looking.

ALECK. I wish you would order some sandwiches for us. I can't stand it any longer. A human being has to eat.

TOURIST (*ecstatically*). What a tragedy!

Katie dear, can you realize it? Consider how awful. The weather is so beautiful, and the chief correspondent. Take out your note-book, Jimmie.

JAMES. I lost it, father.

CORRESPONDENT. Where is he?

VOICES (*obligingly*). There, there he is. There! A little higher. Still higher! A little lower! No, higher!

CORRESPONDENT. If you please, if you please, ladies and gentlemen, I will find him myself. Oh, yes, there he is. Hm! What a situation!

TOURIST. Won't you have a chair?

CORRESPONDENT. Thank you. (*Sits down.*) Hm! What a situation! Very interesting. Very interesting, indeed. (*Whisks out his note-book; amiably to the photographers.*) Have you taken any pictures yet, gentlemen?

FIRST PHOTOGRAPHER. Yes, sir, certainly, certainly. We have photographed the place showing the general character of the locality—

SECOND PHOTOGRAPHER. The tragic situation of the young man—

CORRESPONDENT. Ye-es, very, very interesting.

TOURIST. Did you hear, Aleck? This smart man, the chief correspondent, says it's interesting, and you keep bothering about sandwiches. Dunce!

ALECK. May be he has had his dinner already.

CORRESPONDENT. Ladies and gentlemen, I beg you to be quiet.

OBLIGING VOICES. It is quieter in the café.

CORRESPONDENT (*shouts to the unknown man*). Permit me to introduce myself. I am the chief correspondent of the European press. I have been sent here at the special request of the editors. I should like to ask you several questions concerning your situation. What is your name? What is your general position? How old are you? (*The unknown man mumbles something.*)

CORRESPONDENT (*a little puzzled*). I can't hear a thing. Has he been that way all the time?

VOICES. Yes, it's impossible to hear a word he says.

CORRESPONDENT (*jotting down something in his note-book*). Fine! Are you a bachelor? (*The unknown man mumbles.*)

CORRESPONDENT. I can't hear you. Are you married? Yes?

TOURIST. He said he was a bachelor.

SECOND TOURIST. No, he didn't. Of course, he's married.

CORRESPONDENT (*carelessly*). You think so? All right. We'll put down, married. How many children have you? Can't hear! It seems to me he said three. Hm! Anyway, we'll put down five.

TOURIST. Oh, my, what a tragedy. Five children! Imagine!

MILITARY WOMAN. He is lying.

CORRESPONDENT (*shouting*). How did you get into this position? What? I can't hear? Louder! Repeat. What did you say? (*Perplexed, to the crowd.*) What did he say? The fellow has a devilishly weak voice.

FIRST TOURIST. It seems to me he said that he lost his way.

SECOND TOURIST. No, he doesn't know himself how he got there.

VOICES. He was out hunting.—He was climbing up the rocks.—No, no! He is simply a lunatic!

CORRESPONDENT. I beg your pardon, I beg your pardon, ladies and gentlemen! Anyway, he didn't drop from the sky. However— (*He quickly jots down in his note-book.*) Unhappy young man—suffering from childhood with attacks of lunacy.—The bright light of the full moon—the wild rocks.—Sleepy janitor—didn't notice—

FIRST TOURIST (*to the second, in a whisper*). But it's new moon now.

SECOND TOURIST. Go, what does a layman know about astronomy.

TOURIST (*ecstatically*). Mary, pay attention to this! You have before you an ocular demonstration of the influence of the moon on living organisms. What a terrible tragedy to go out walking on a moonlit night and find suddenly that you have climbed to a place whence it is impossible to climb down or be taken down.

CORRESPONDENT (*shouting*). What feelings are you experiencing? I can't hear. Louder! Ah, so? Well, well! What a situation!

CROWD (*interested*). Listen, listen! Let's hear what his feelings are. How terrible!

CORRESPONDENT (*writes in his note-book, tossing out detached remarks*). Mortal terror numbs his limbs.—A cold shiver goes down his spinal column.—No hope.—Before his mental vision rises a picture of family bliss: Wife making sandwiches; his five children innocently lisping their love.—Grandma in the arm-chair with a tube to her ear, that is, grandpa in the arm-chair, with a tube to *his* ear and grandma.—Deeply moved by the sympathy of the public.—His last wish before his death that the words he uttered with his last breath should be published in our newspapers—

MILITARY WOMAN (*indignantly*). My! He lies like a salesman.

MARY (*wearily*). Papa, children, look, he is starting to fall again.

TOURIST (*angrily*). Don't bother me. Such a

tragedy is unfolding itself right before your very eyes—and you— What are you making such big eyes for again?

CORRESPONDENT (*shouting*). Hold on fast. That's it! My last question: What message do you wish to leave for your fellow citizens before you depart for the better world?

UNKNOWN MAN. That they may all go to the devil.

CORRESPONDENT. What? Hm, yes— (*He writes quickly.*) Ardent love—is a stanch opponent of the law granting equal rights to negroes. His last words: "Let the black niggers—"

PASTOR (*out of breath, pushing through the crowd*). Where is he? Ah, there! Poor young man. Has there been no clergyman here yet? No? Thank you. Am I the first?

CORRESPONDENT (*writes*). A touching dramatic moment.—A minister has arrived.—All are trembling on the verge of suspense. Many are shedding tears—

PASTOR. Excuse me, excuse me! Ladies and gentlemen, a lost soul wishes to make its peace with God— (*He shouts.*) My son, don't you wish to make your peace with God? Confess your sins to me. I will grant you remission at once! What? I cannot hear?

CORRESPONDENT (*writes*). The air is shaken with the people's groans. The minister of the church exhorts the criminal, that is, the unfortunate man, in touching language.—The unfortunate creature with tears in his eyes thanks him in a faint voice—

UNKNOWN MAN (*faintly*). If you won't go away I will jump on your head. I weigh three hundred pounds. (*All jump away frightened behind each other.*)

VOICES. He is falling! He is falling!

TOURIST (*agitatingly*). Mary, Aleck, Jimmie.

POLICEMAN (*energetically*). Clear the place, please! Move on!

LADY. Nellie, go quick and tell your father he is falling.

PHOTOGRAPHER (*in despair*). Oh my, I am out of films (*tosses madly about, looking pitifully at the unknown man*). One minute, I'll go and get them. I have some in my overcoat pocket over there. (*He walks a short distance, keeping his eyes fixed on the unknown man, and then returns.*) I can't, I am afraid I'll miss it. Good heavens! They are over there in my overcoat. Just one minute, please. I'll fetch them right away. What a fix.

PASTOR. Hurry, my friend. Pull yourself together and try to hold out long enough to tell me at least your principal sins. You needn't mention the lesser ones.

TOURIST. What a tragedy?

CORRESPONDENT (*writes*). The criminal, that is, the unhappy man, makes a public confession and does pennance. Terrible secrets revealed. He is a bank robber—blew up safes.

TOURIST (*credulously*). The scoundrel.

PASTOR (*shouts*). In the first place, have you killed? Secondly, have you stolen? Thirdly, have you committed adultery?

TOURIST. Mary, Jimmie, Katie, Aleck, Charlie, close your ears.

CORRESPONDENT (*writing*). Tremendous excitement in the crowd.—Shouts of indignation.

PASTOR (*hurriedly*). Fourthly, have you blasphemed? Fifthly, have you coveted your neighbor's ass, his ox, his slave, his wife? Sixthly—

PHOTOGRAPHER (*alarmed*). Ladies and gentlemen, an ass!

SECOND PHOTOGRAPHER. Where? I can't see it!

PHOTOGRAPHER (*calmed*). I thought I heard it.

PASTOR. I congratulate you, my son! I congratulate you! You have made your peace with God. Now you may rest easy—Oh, God, what do

I see? The Salvation Army! Policeman, chase them away!

(*Enter a Salvation Army band, men and women in uniforms. There are only three instruments, a drum, a violin and a piercingly shrill trumpet.*)

SALVATION ARMY MAN (*frantically beating his drum and shouting in a nasal voice*). Brethren and sisters—

PASTOR (*shouting even louder in a still more nasal voice in an effort to drown the other's*). He has already confessed. Bear witness, ladies and gentlemen, that he has confessed and made his peace with heaven.

SALVATION ARMY WOMAN (*climbing on a rock and shrieking*). I once wandered in the dark just as this sinner and I lived a bad life and was a drunkard, but when the light of truth—

A VOICE. Why, she is drunk now.

PASTOR. Policeman, didn't he confess and make his peace with heaven?

(*The Salvation Army man continues to beat his drum frantically; the rest begin to drawl a song. Shouts, laughter, whistling. Singing in the café, and calls of "Waiter!" in all languages. The bewildered policemen tear themselves away from the pastor, who is pulling them somewhere; the photographers turn and twist about as if the seats*) *were burning under them. An English lady comes riding in on a donkey, who, stopping suddenly, sprawls out his legs and refuses to go farther, adding his noise to the rest. Gradually the noise subsides. The Salvation Army band solemnly withdraws, and the pastor, waving his hands, follows them.)*

FIRST ENGLISH TOURIST (*to the other*). How impolite! This crowd doesn't know how to behave itself.

SECOND ENGLISH TOURIST. Come, let's go away from here.

FIRST ENGLISH TOURIST. One minute. (*He shouts.*) Listen, won't you hurry up and fall?

SECOND ENGLISH TOURIST. What are you saying, Sir William?

FIRST ENGLISH TOURIST (*shouting*). Don't you see that's what they are waiting for? As a gentleman you should grant them this pleasure and so escape the humiliation of undergoing tortures before this mob.

SECOND ENGLISH TOURIST. Sir William.

TOURIST (*ecstatically*). See? It's true. Aleck, Jimmie, it's true. What a tragedy!

SEVERAL TOURISTS (*going for the Englishman*). How dare you?

FIRST ENGLISH TOURIST (*shoving them aside*).

Hurry up and fall! Do you hear? If you haven't the backbone I'll help you out with a pistol shot.

VOICES. That red-haired devil has gone clear out of his mind.

POLICEMAN (*seizing the Englishman's hand*). You have no right to do it, it's against the law. I'll arrest you.

SOME TOURISTS. A barbarous nation!

(*The unknown man shouts something. Excitement below.*)

VOICES. Hear, hear, hear!

UNKNOWN MAN (*aloud*). Take that jackass away to the devil. He wants to shoot me. And tell the boss that I can't stand it any longer.

VOICES. What's that? What boss? He is losing his mind, the poor man.

TOURIST. Aleck! Mary! This is a mad scene. Jimmie, you remember Hamlet? Quick.

UNKNOWN MAN (*angrily*). Tell him my spinal column is broken.

MARY (*wearily*). Papa, children, he's beginning to kick with his legs.

KATE. Is that what is called convulsions, papa?

TOURIST (*rapturously*). I don't know. I think it is. What a tragedy?

ALECK (*glumly*). You fool! You keep cramming and cramming and you don't know that the right name for that is agony. And you wear eyeglasses, too. I can't bear it any longer, papa.

TOURIST. Think of it, children. A man is about to fall down to his death and he is bothering about his spinal column.

(*There is a noise. A man in a white vest, very much frightened, enters, almost dragged by angry tourists. He smiles, bows on all sides, stretches out his arms, now running forward as he is pushed, now trying to escape in the crowd, but is seized and pulled again.*)

VOICES. A bare-faced deception! It is an outrage. Policeman, policeman, he must be taught a lesson!

OTHER VOICES. What is it? What deception? What is it all about? They have caught a thief!

THE MAN IN THE WHITE VEST (*bowing and smiling*). It's a joke, ladies and gentlemen, a joke, that's all. The people were bored, so I wanted to provide a little amusement for them.

UNKNOWN MAN (*angrily*). Boss!

THE MAN IN THE WHITE VEST. Wait a while, wait a while.

UNKNOWN MAN. Do you expect me to stay here until the Second Advent? The agreement was till twelve o'clock. What time is it now?

TALL TOURIST (*indignantly*). Do you hear,

ladies and gentlemen? This scoundrel, this man here in the white vest hired that other scoundrel up there and just simply tied him to the rock.

VOICES. Is he tied?

TALL TOURIST. Yes, he is tied and he can't fall. We are excited and worrying, but he couldn't fall even if he tried.

UNKNOWN MAN. What else do you want? Do you think I am going to break my neck for your measly ten dollars? Boss, I can't stand it any more. One man wanted to shoot me. The pastor preached me for two hours. This is not in the agreement.

ALECK. Father, I told you that Baedecker lies. You believe everything anybody tells you and drag us about without eating.

MAN IN THE WHITE VEST. The people were bored. My only desire was to amuse the people.

MILITARY WOMAN. What is the matter? I don't understand a thing. Why isn't he going to fall? Who, then, is going to fall?

TOURIST. I don't understand a thing either. Of course he's got to fall!

JAMES. You never understand anything, father. Weren't you told that he's tied to the rock?

ALECK. You can't convince him. He loves every Baedecker more than his own children.

JAMES. A nice father!

TOURIST. Silence!

MILITARY WOMAN. What is the matter? He must fall.

TALL TOURIST. The idea! What a deception. You'll have to explain this.

MAN IN THE WHITE VEST. The people were bored. Excuse me, ladies and gentlemen, but wishing to accommodate you—give you a few hours of pleasant excitement—elevate your spirits—inspire you with altruistic sentiments—

ENGLISHMAN. Is the café yours?

MAN IN THE WHITE VEST. Yes.

ENGLISHMAN. And is the hotel below also yours?

GENTLEMAN. Yes. The people were bored—

CORRESPONDENT (*writing*). The proprietor of the café, desiring to increase his profits from the sale of alcoholic beverages, exploits the best human sentiments.—The people's indignation—

UNKNOWN MAN (*angrily*). Boss, will you have me taken off at once or won't you?

HOTEL KEEPER. What do you want up there? Aren't you satisfied? Didn't I have you taken off at night?

UNKNOWN MAN. Well, I should say so. You think I'd be hanging here nights, too!

HOTEL OWNER. Then you can stand it a few minutes longer. The people are bored—

TALL TOURIST. Say, have you any idea of what you have done? Do you realize the enormity of it? You are scoundrels, who for your own sordid personal ends have impiously exploited the finest human sentiment, love of one's neighbor. You have caused us to undergo fear and suffering. You have poisoned our hearts with pity. And now, what is the upshot of it all? The upshot is that this scamp, your vile accomplice, is bound to the rock and not only will he not fall as everybody expects, but he *can't*.

MILITARY WOMAN. What is the matter? He has got to fall.

TOURIST. Policeman! Policeman!

(*The pastor enters, out of breath.*)

PASTOR. What? Is he still living? Oh, there he is! What fakirs those Salvationists are.

VOICES. Don't you know that he is bound?

PASTOR. Bound! Bound to what? To life? Well, we are all bound to life until death snaps the cord. But whether he is bound or not bound, I reconciled him with heaven, and that's enough. But those fakirs—

TOURIST. Policeman! Policeman, you must

draw up an official report. There is no way out of it.

MILITARY WOMAN (*going for the hotel owner*). I will not allow myself to be fooled. I saw an aeronaut drop from the clouds and go crash upon a roof. I saw a tiger tear a woman to pieces—

PHOTOGRAPHER. I spoiled three films photographing that scamp. You will have to answer for this, sir. I will hold you responsible.

TOURIST. An official report! An official report! Such a bare-faced deception. Mary, Jimmie, Aleck, Charlie, call a policeman.

HOTEL KEEPER (*drawing back, in despair*). But, I can't make him fall if he doesn't want to. I did everything in my power, ladies and gentlemen!

MILITARY WOMAN. I will not allow it.

HOTEL KEEPER. Excuse me. I promise you on my word of honor that the next time he will fall. But he doesn't want to, to-day.

UNKNOWN MAN. What's that? What did you say about the next time?

HOTEL KEEPER. You shut up there!

UNKNOWN MAN. For ten dollars?

PASTOR. Pray, what impudence! I just made his peace with heaven when he was in danger of his life. You have heard him threatening to fall on my head, haven't you? And still he is dissatisfied.

Adulterer, thief, murderer, coveter of your neighbor's ass—

PHOTOGRAPHER. Ladies and gentlemen, an ass!

SECOND PHOTOGRAPHER. Where, where is an ass?

PHOTOGRAPHER (*calmed*). I thought I heard one.

SECOND PHOTOGRAPHER. It is you who are an ass. I have become cross-eyed on account of your shouting: "An ass! An ass!"

MARY (*wearily*). Papa, children, look! A policeman is coming.

(*Excitement and noise. On one side a crowd pulling a policeman, on the other the hotel keeper; both keep crying: "Excuse me! Excuse me!"*)

TOURIST. Policeman, there he is, the fakir, the swindler.

PASTOR. Policeman, there he is, the adulterer, the murderer, the coveter of his neighbor's ass—

POLICEMAN. Excuse me, excuse me, ladies and gentlemen. We will bring him to his senses in short order and make him confess.

HOTEL KEEPER. I can't make him fall if he doesn't want to.

POLICEMAN. Hey, you, young man out there! Can you fall or can't you? Confess!

UNKNOWN MAN (*sullenly*). I don't want to fall!

VOICES. Aha, he has confessed. What a scoundrel!

TALL TOURIST. Write down what I dictate, policeman— "Desiring—for the sake of gain to exploit the sentiment of love of one's neighbor— the sacred feeling—a-a-a—"

TOURIST. Listen children, they are drawing up an official report. What exquisite choice of language!

TALL TOURIST. The sacred feeling which—

POLICEMAN (*writing with painful effort, his tongue stuck out.*) Love of one's neighbor—the sacred feeling which—

MARY (*wearily*). Papa, children, look! An advertisement is coming.

(*Enter musicians with trumpets and drums, a man at their head carrying on a long pole a huge placard with the picture of an absolutely bald head, and printed underneath: "I was bald."*)

UNKNOWN MAN. Too late. They are drawing up a report here. You had better skidoo!

THE MAN CARRYING THE POLE (*stopping and speaking in a loud voice*). I had been bald from the day of my birth and for a long time thereafter. That miserable growth, which in my tenth year covered my scalp was more like wool than real hair. When I was married my skull was as bare as a pillow and my young bride—

TOURIST. What a tragedy! Newly married and with such a head! Can you realize how dreadful that is, children?

(*All listen with interest, even the policeman stopping in his arduous task and inclining his ear with his pen in his hand.*)

THE MAN CARRYING THE POLE (*solemnly*). And the time came when my matrimonial happiness literally hung by a hair. All the medicines recommended by quacks to make my hair grow—

TOURIST. Your note-book, Jimmie.

MILITARY WOMAN. But when is he going to fall?

HOTEL KEEPER (*amiably*). The next time, lady, the next time. I won't tie him so hard—you understand?

(CURTAIN.)